WITHDRAWN

Dedicated with love to

Phineas Holeman

—Serena Valentino

Copyright © 2022 Disney Enterprises, Inc.

All rights reserved. Published by Disney Press,

an imprint of Buena Vista Books, Inc.

No part of this book may be reproduced or transmitted

in any form or by any means, electronic or mechanical,

including photocopying, recording, or by any information

storage and retrieval system, without written permission

from the publisher. For information address Disney Press,

1200 Grand Central Avenue, Glendale, California 91201.

Printed in the United States of America

First Hardcover Edition, September 2022

1 3 5 7 9 10 8 6 4 2

FAC-034274-22203

Library of Congress Control Number: 2021949248

ISBN 978-1-368-07701-9

Visit www.disneybooks.com

Disney

HOW THE VILLAINS RUINED
CHRISTMAS

WITHDRAWN

Written by *New York Times* best-selling author

Serena Valentino

Illustrated by **Joey Chou**

Disney PRESS

Los Angeles • New York

All around the world children squealed with delight.
"Christmas is coming," they said with smiles so bright.

Out came the lights, the stockings, and the tree,
filling their hearts and imaginations with glee.

Meanwhile the villains seethed in their ominous dwellings,
ranting and raving, their anger swelling.

They all despised this beloved season,
each one for a different reason.

Every Christmas Maleficent sent her raven spy,
who flew through the kingdom like a magical eye.

He brought her word of a gala affair,
but no invitation, to her great despair.

Hades sulked on his Underworld throne,
his head aflame, and with an angry tone,
declared he had no patience for mortals this year
and wished to diminish their excessive good cheer.

As Captain Hook sailed through the Never Land sea,
he had visions of Lost Boys on a rambunctious spree,
all in a tizzy over their holiday treasure
and causing much havoc, to Hook's deep displeasure.

The Queen's pretty face twisted into a sneer as she looked with disgust into her magic mirror.

She loathed the admiration Christmas received.
It made her quite cross and assuredly peeved.

In her undersea realm Ursula let out a groan
at the thought of King Triton happy on his throne,
watching the merfolk swim and sing
and make merry with their beloved king.

Cruella sat wickedly inside Hell Hall,
still bitter over her unfortunate downfall.
The holidays reminded her of plans gone wrong,
and she was still offended by Roger's song.

The villains decided something must be done

to put an end to the holiday fun.

Maleficent sent her goons to the celebration,
hoping they'd cause a horrendous vexation:
ruining the feast, disrupting the dance,
and smashing the gifts with a laugh and a prance.

Hades conjured his magical flame
and set the tree ablaze in his name.

As the branches ignited, the mortals' eyes grew big,
which made Hades laugh and dance a jig.

To prevent the Lost Boys' excessive joy
upon unwrapping their Christmas toys,
Hook tossed their gifts into the ocean,
hoping to stop the expected commotion.

The Queen poisoned the apples for the holiday pies
and thought she'd bring them round as a delightful surprise.

UNHAPPINESS HAPPINESS

She smiled and left, her plan now in motion.
The Dwarfs would succumb to her unhappiness potion.

The ocean bubbled like a witch's pot,
bringing forth Ursula's terrible plot.
The water swirled into a menacing cyclone,
threatening to sweep Triton right off his throne.

Cruella recruited Jasper and Horace
to dress up as carolers and sing a chorus.
They would distract with a musical number
while she snuck in during the Dalmatians' slumber.

But despite every effort by our dastardly friends,
they could not bring this holiday to an end.

At the party, Maleficent's goons joined the reverie
and passed out the presents from under the tree.

Hades's grand plans fell into despair
while he watched his flames flutter and flair.
The mortals had gathered around the pyre
to roast marshmallows with his fire!

The Lost Boys loved Hook's latest stunt,
for he had gifted them a scavenger hunt!

The Queen's apple pies lacked their desired notion.
By mistake, she'd concocted a happiness potion.

Ursula's spell, to her disappointment,
only served to add to the king's enjoyment.

Jasper and Horace sang with all their might,
waking the puppies with such a delight,

which left Cruella to play Santa Claus,
forced to be covered in slobber and paws.

May this be a lesson to villains far and near:
Christmas isn't a time for causing fear.
Holiday spirit cannot be diminished,
though I have an inkling our friends aren't quite finished.
They are villains, dear readers, this is abundantly true,
and what else is a villain expected to do?

31901068746504